Jack and the Beanstalk

Manufactured in the U.S.A.

8 7 6 5 4 3 2 1

ISBN 1-56173-914-6

Cover illustration by Sam Thiewes

Book illustrations by Susan Spellman

Story adapted by Jane Jerrard

HTS BOOKS
AN IMPRINT OF FOREST HOUSE™
School & Library Edition

ong ago, there lived a poor woman and her son named Jack. They had no money and no food, so the woman decided that they must sell their milking cow.

The woman asked Jack to take the cow into town and offer it for sale. But on the road into town, Jack met a strange old man who asked to buy the cow.

"I will give you five magic beans for your cow," he told Jack. "Do you know how many that is?"

"Two in each hand and one in my mouth!" answered Jack.

"Right!" said the old man, "and here are the five beans." So Jack traded the cow for the five magic beans.

hen Jack returned home, he proudly told his mother of the good trade he had made.

"You foolish boy!" she said. "Now we must go hungry!" And she threw the beans out the window, for she did not believe they were magic at all. Then she sent Jack to bed without any supper—though there was nothing to eat anyway.

The next morning, Jack awoke to find a giant beanstalk growing from the ground where the beans had fallen. It was so tall, it grew all the way up to the sky!

Jack climbed up the beanstalk until he reached the clouds. He kept climbing until he was above the clouds. And there before him, he saw a great castle.

ack walked up to the castle door. There, in the doorway, stood the biggest woman that he had ever seen!

"Please, Ma'am, I am hungry. Could I come in and have something to eat?" asked Jack.

The woman said that her husband, who was also a giant, was coming home soon and would want to eat Jack for his supper. But Jack asked again so nicely that the woman brought him inside and gave him some breakfast.

No sooner had Jack finished eating than he heard the *tramp, tramp, tramp* of the Giant's boots.

Quick as a wink, the woman popped Jack into the unlit oven, safely out of sight.

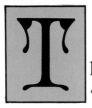he Giant filled the kitchen door and roared,
"Fe fi fo fum,
 I smell the blood of an Englishman!
Be he live or be he dead,
 I'll grind his bones to make my bread!"

"You only smell the stew I have cooked," said his wife, setting a huge bowl in front of him.

After the Giant had eaten his fill, he called for his gold. His wife brought his bags full of gold coins. The Giant counted the coins until he grew sleepy. His head nodded and he began to snore.

Jack slipped out of the dark oven and grabbed one of the bags of gold. Then he ran as fast as he could to the beanstalk and climbed down.

is mother was happy to have him home, and the gold bought them food for months. But as soon as the coins were spent, Jack disguised himself and again climbed the beanstalk up past the clouds, and asked the Giant's wife to let him into the castle.

The woman did not recognize Jack in his disguise. But she did not want to let him in. She told Jack that the last boy she let in to feed had stolen some of her husband's gold.

But Jack asked so nicely for a drink that she brought him to the kitchen and gave him a thimble of water.

No sooner had Jack finished the water than he heard the tramping of giant boots and ran to hide in the oven. The Giant roared,

> "Fe fi fo fum,
>   I smell the blood of an Englishman!
> Be he live or be he dead,
>   I'll grind his bones to make my bread!"

His wife said, "You only smell this delicious soup I have cooked for you." Then she fed the Giant his supper.

After the Giant had eaten, he called to his wife and told her to bring his hen.

"Lay an egg!" commanded the Giant. The hen laid a perfect, golden egg. Soon the Giant fell asleep and Jack crept out from his hiding place. He grabbed the wonderful hen, and did not stop running until he was safely home.

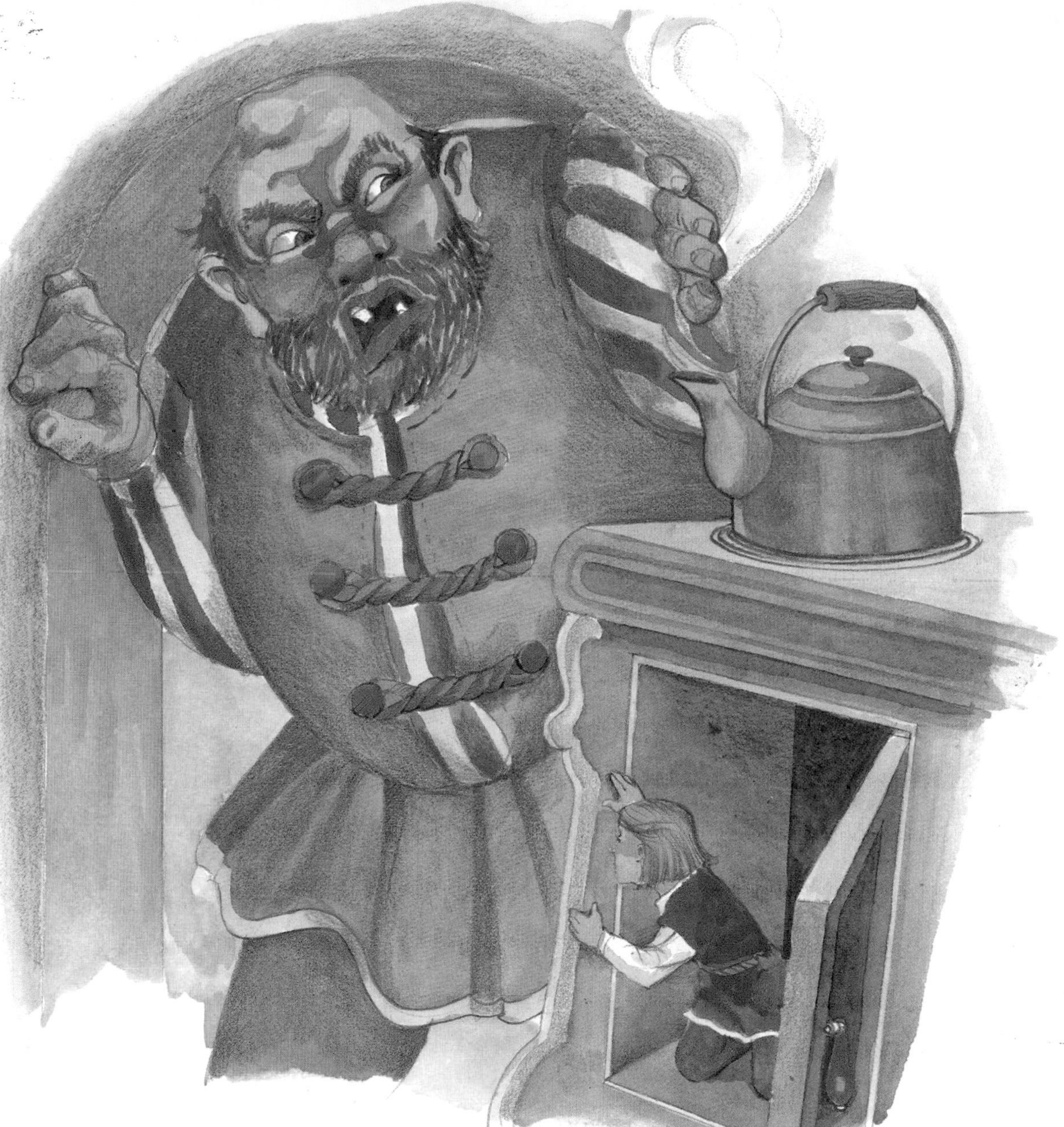

Each day the hen laid a golden egg, so Jack and his mother were able to sell them to buy plenty of food to eat. Jack's mother was very happy.

But Jack still longed for adventure. So he climbed up the beanstalk once more and tiptoed into the Giant's castle. He hid in the kitchen behind a giant broom.

Soon the Giant and his wife came in. The Giant looked around and cried,

"Fe fi fo fum,
    I smell the blood of an . . ."

His wife ran to look in the oven, but no one was there.

he Giant sat down in his chair with a thump that rattled the kitchen floor, and called for his wife to bring him his magic harp. Jack watched as a lovely golden harp was set before the Giant.

When the Giant roared, "Sing!" the harp played a beautiful song all by itself. It even sang along with its music in a soft, sweet voice. The Giant ate his supper while the harp played and sang. And when the Giant was full, the harp's music lulled the Giant to sleep.

When the giant was snoring loudly, and was most certainly asleep, Jack crept from his hiding place behind the huge broom. He grabbed the golden harp and ran away with it.

he magic harp called out, "Help, Master!"

This woke the sleeping Giant. When he realized that his prized harp was being stolen, the Giant leaped up with a mighty roar of rage and tried to grab Jack with his giant hand.

Jack jumped off the table and ran just as fast as his legs would carry him. He could hear the *tramp, tramp, tramp* of the Giant's boots behind him, and that made Jack run faster than he had ever run before!

When he reached the beanstalk, Jack quickly climbed all the way down to the ground with the magic harp clutched tightly in one arm.

As soon as Jack reached the ground, he grabbed an axe and, with one sharp blow, chopped down the beanstalk. Down it crashed, and with it crashed the Giant.

That was the end of the magic beanstalk, and that was the end of the Giant!

As for Jack and his mother, they lived happily ever after with the wonderful hen and the magical golden harp.